Meet the Author

www.darylcobb.com

Daryl Cobb lives in New Jersey with his family, not far from his home town. Daryl's writing began in college as a Theatre Arts major at Virginia Commonwealth University. He found a freshman writing class inspiring and, combined with his love for music and the guitar, he discovered a passion for songwriting. This talent would motivate him for years to come and the rhythm he created with his music also found its way into the bedtime stories he later created for his children. The story "Boy on the Hill," about a boy who turns the clouds into animals, was his first bedtime story/song and was inspired by his son and an infatuation with the shapes of clouds. Through the years his son and daughter have inspired so much of his work, including "Daniel Dinosaur" and "Daddy Did I Ever Say? I Love You, Love You, Every Day."

Daryl spends a lot of his time these days visiting schools promoting literacy with his interactive educational assemblies "Teaching Through Creative Arts." These performance programs teach children about the writing and creative process and allow Daryl to do what he feels is most important -- inspire children to read and write. He also performs at benefits and libraries with his "Music & Storytime" shows.

He is a member of the SCBWI.

Meet the Illustrator
www.piedenero.com

Manuela Pentangelo lives in Busnago, Italy, near Milan, with her flowers, family and friends. She was born in Holland, but has lived all of her life in Italy. A student of architectural design, Manuela discovered that her dreams and goals lay elsewhere. She likes to say that she was born with a pencil in her hand, but it took a while before she realized that her path was to illustrate for children. Manuela often visits London, where she likes to sketch at the British Museum, and likes traveling to different places to find inspiration.

She is a member of the SCBWI.

Printed in the USA
10to2childrensbooks.com

Greta's Magical Mistake

Written by Daryl K. Cobb

Illustrated by Manuela Pentangelo

10 To 2 Children's Books / Clinton

ISBN 978-0615796321

Written by Daryl K. Cobb
Illustrated by Manuela Pentangelo

10 To 2 Children's Books

Time to Read

™

First Printing 2011

Cameron and Kayley

Always be kind to others and find it in your hearts to be forgiving! We all make mistakes and I hope you will both learn from them and become better people because of them.

Dad
(aka Daryl K. Cobb)

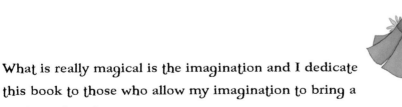

What is really magical is the imagination and I dedicate this book to those who allow my imagination to bring a smile to their face.

Manuela Pentangelo

"Wilhelm's Magic Academy"
the sign read near the door.

They train the magically gifted,
witches, warlocks and more.

Finishing up her second year
was little Greta Grohm.
She left the school in the pouring rain
to make her way back home.

Greta heard a purring sound,
despite a passing train.
She saw the cat beneath a car,
hiding from the rain.

"Kitty, Kitty, what's your name?"
The cat heard her say.
"I have two friends at home
who would love to play."

Greta scooped the kitty up
and put him in her bag.
The cat was all alone and
had no collar and no tag.

"I will name you Hamlet.
I think that sounds quite nice."

Then she walked into her home
and she called out twice,

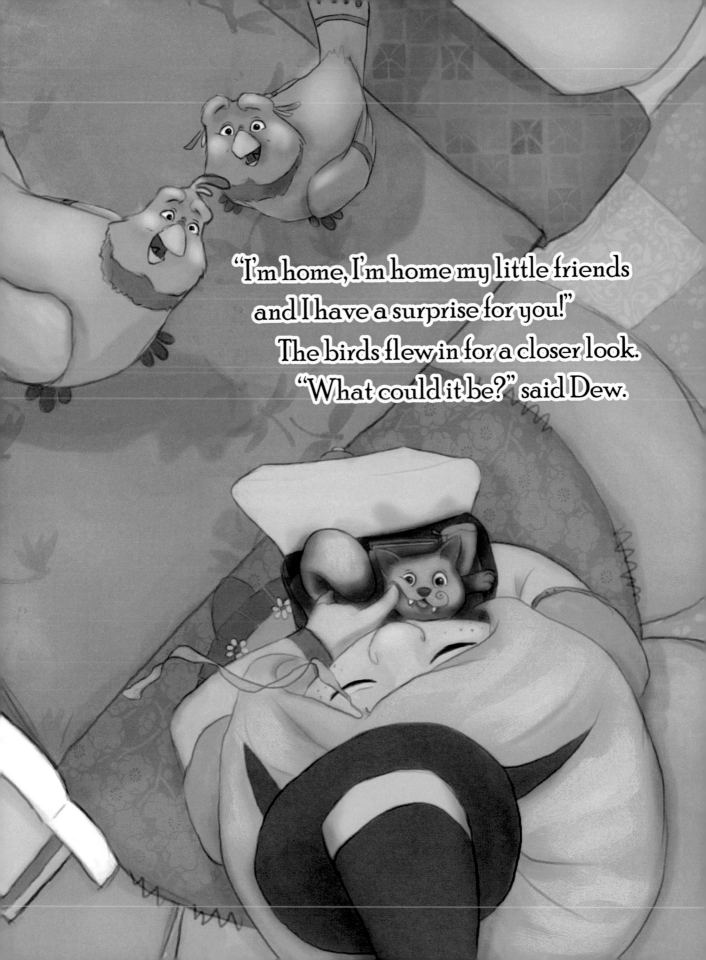

"I'm home, I'm home my little friends
and I have a surprise for you!"
The birds flew in for a closer look.
"What could it be?" said Dew.

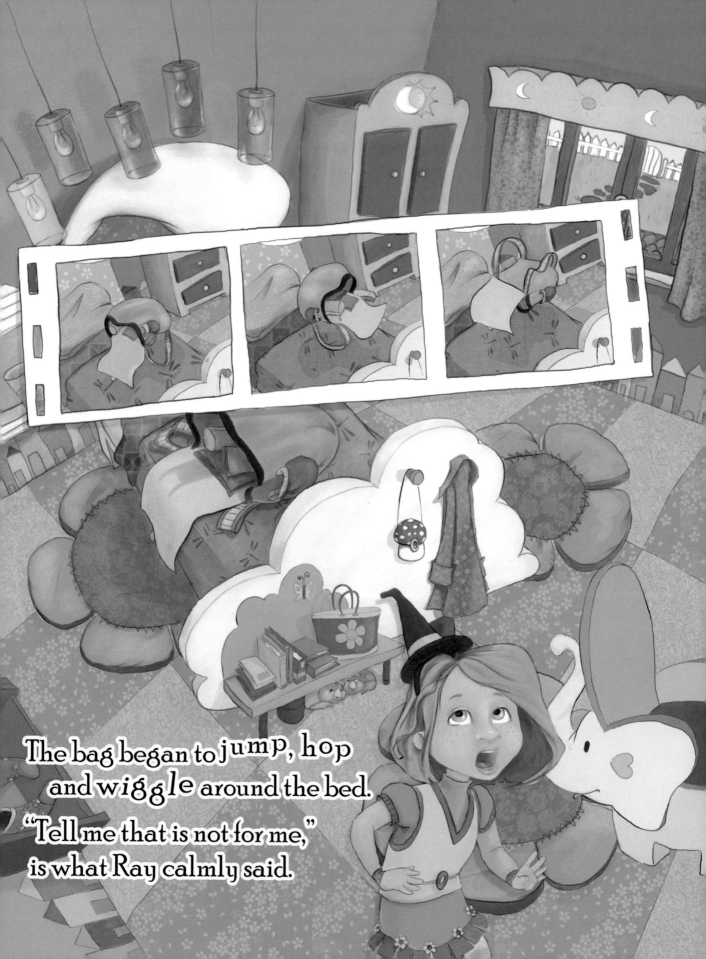

The bag began to jump, hop
and wiggle around the bed.

"Tell me that is not for me,"
is what Ray calmly said.

Hamlet peeked
out of Greta's bag
with a very scary look.

Ray and Dew both *screamed* out loud
as the cat hissed and sh o o k.

Dew and Ray flapped their wings
and Hamlet hissed some more.
Hamlet jumped into the air
and landed on the floor.

He ran around the room,
then jumped up on a chair,
from there he leaped onto the desk
and back into the air.

Greta followed right behind, her magic wand in hand,

screaming out a little spell,

"Cala-figgy-mand."

The room went oddly silent.
You could not hear a sound,

and her newest friend, Hamlet,
was nowhere to be found.

"Hamlet, Hamlet!
Where did he go?"
Dew said to Ray,
"I do not know."

Then Greta noticed
something move
in the painting on the wall.

She started feeling
slightly faint
and thought that
she might fall.

"Hamlet!" she screamed in complete surprise.
He was sitting right there in front of her eyes!

In a field of sunflowers,
now looking rather small,
Hamlet sat and waved at them.
They even heard him call.

"Oh my, oh my,
what have I done?"
you could hear her say.

Ray then laughed
and said to Dew,
"He looks so nice that way."

"Stop it, stop it, both of you.
We must bring him home.
We can not just leave him there
lost and all alone.

Wilhelm's book of magic spells
will tell me what to do."

"Oh, no," said Ray,
"not the book!"
He frowned
and looked at Dew.

Greta opened up the book
and a voice said,

"What is it now!

Did you turn your mom
into a dog, or the
dog into a cow?"

Greta explained in great detail
all that she had done.

"Cala-figgy-mand?"
said the book,
"That spell's an easy one.

To reverse this spell
repeat it once,
then repeat it and
tap your shoe.

Now listen, Greta, you must beware
of what I say to you..."

But before the book could finish,
Greta said the magic word.
"Cala-figgy-mand" was all the birds had heard.

Then everything turned yellow
and they slammed into a tree.

They woke up on the ground in a sea of golden leaves.

Dew asked, "Ray are you ok?"
"I am not sure just yet.
How about you?" Ray said to Dew.
"I think I need a vet.

"I'm feeling rather dizzy.
I am not okay at all,
and look at us! We're stuck here
in the painting on the wall!"

"Ray and Dew, I'm sorry!
What did I do wrong?
I think between 'Cal' and 'fig'
I may have paused too long."

Ray replied in an angry tone,
"Repeat, repeat it said.
That meant twice,
we heard the book.
You said it once instead."

Greta's eyes filled with tears.
Ray knew that she felt bad.
"Everyone makes mistakes," she said.
"Please, don't be mad."

They flew onto her shoulders,
Ray kissed her with his beak.
Dew then wiped a tear away
as it rolled down her cheek.

Hamlet watched them comfort her
from behind a sunflower tree.

Then he said to everyone,
"Did you really come for *me?*"

Greta's reply was soft and slow,
"Did you really think we'd let you go?"

A smile appeared from ear to ear
on Hamlet's furry face.
He now knew that in Greta's heart
he had found his place.

"Please come **home**," said Ray and Dew.
"We really want to play with you."

"It is time for me to fix this spell,"
said little Gretta Grohm,
"and take us all back safe and sound
to our comfy home."

Dew, Ray and Hamlet
closed their eyes real tight,
hoping that Greta
would somehow get it right.

She flicked her wrist
and waived her hand,
"Cala-figgy-mand,
cala-figgy-mand."

Then like clouds in the sky they just floated along,

going up and up, until *poof,* they were gone.

With one big **b o u n c e**
they landed safely in bed.

"I need to listen better
and practice," Greta said.

They all became one family
on this happy day,

and on this day every year,
in those yellow fields they play.

Pirates: The Ring of Hope

"Cobb's 14th book comes complete with pirates, mysterious messages and a magic ring . . .. The characters are rich and beautifully rendered, and the story is sprinkled with humor . . .. Much of the dialogue is delightfully silly. . . . [A] spirited swashbuckling tale of mystery and magic."

-- Kirkus Reviews

Mr. Moon

"A pleasing children's narrative with a relevant message. ... Cobb's text ... has a simple charm likely to please young readers [and]. . . Jaeger's illustrations give the night a soft, beautiful glow, complementing Cobb's text . . .. Her personifications of Mr. Moon and Mr. Sun are utterly delightful."

-- Kirkus Reviews

Daddy Did I Ever Say? I Love You, Love You, Every Day

"A cute, curly-haired, kindergarten-aged girl opens the story by asking her father if she's ever told him how much she loves him . . . the sentiment is sweet and Van Wagoner's illustrations are eye catching. . .. The verse Cobb has penned is appealing and . . . [t]he idea behind the story of the little girl and her doting father is charming[.] " -- Kirkus Reviews

Daniel Dinosaur

"A sweet story told in simple rhymes that young children will likely enjoy. Cobb and Castangno's cute, colorful picture book illustrates the bond between a brother and sister." -- Kirkus Reviews

Bill the Bat Baby Sits Bella

"A sweet book celebrating brother-sister bonds."
-- Kirkus Reviews

Bill the Bat Loves Halloween

"A fast- moving, fun rhyming picture book . . .."
-- Kirkus Reviews

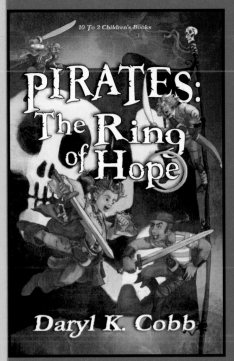

Made in the USA
Lexington, KY
22 March 2018